JAME... ...WEL

By Appointment to
Children's Imagination

Albert Mouse

DARTMOUTH's
MOST FA-MOUSE
EXPLORER

Albert's Christmas Adventure

Albert's Christmas Adventure

The Adventures of Albert Mouse
Book 7

James Hywel

OINK
BOOKS

Books by James Hywel

By Appointment to
children's imagination
www.jameshywel.com

The Milliner Series

The Musings of the Milliner

The Ponderings of the Milliner

The Ruminations of the Milliner

The Cogitations of the Milliner

The Meditations of the Milliner

The Mutterings of the Milliner

The Memories of the Milliner

The Official Mr Milliner Song & Rhyme Book

The Adventures of Albert Mouse Series

The Mouse who wanted to see the World

Albert and the smuggler Mickey Mustard

Albert takes to the sky

Albert and the runaway train

Albert buys a boat

Albert learns to swim

Albert's Christmas Adventure

Other books & short stories

The farmer who overslept

The real reason Trolls are so grumpy

Walk with me

The Elf and the Little Unicorn

First published 2022 by Oink Books
Text Copyright © 2022 by James Hywel
This edition is published in Great Britain
By
Oink Books (James Hywel Books)
The Henley Building
Newtown Road
Henley-on-Thames
Oxfordshire RG9 1ED
England

ISBN 979-8367997415 (paperback)
ISBN 979-8215817810 (ebook)

Printed and bound in Great Britain
This book has been published using Dyslexia
Friendly Font

Written for

Morgan and Josie
and
Mr Spike

'Cherub Cottage' No. 10 Higher
Street, Dartmouth

Chapter 1

Albert Mouse was sitting on the sofa reading a book about woodwork that Mrs Saunders had loaned him from the bookshop.

"Mum, do you think I could have a workshop?" he asked, looking up from the book.

Mrs Mouse put her knitting down and looked at her son over the rim of her glasses.

"A workshop? What kind of workshop?" she asked, sounding slightly concerned.

"You know, with a workbench and

tools so I can make things out of wood?" sighed the little mouse.

"Tools! No, Albert, that sounds like it could be dangerous if you ask me," said his mother.

"But I could make all sorts of things, like furniture and toys," said Albert.

"And a new brain," giggled Dorothy.

Albert threw his sister one of his angry looks.

"It's a lovely idea, Albert, but we don't really have the room for a workshop and I'm not really sure we need any more furniture, do we?" said Mrs Mouse.

Albert returned to reading his book.

Mrs Mouse went back to her knitting but glanced suspiciously over her glasses at her son.

Chapter 2

After lunch, Albert and his sisters helped their mother with the washing up.

"I'm going to sit in the garden and read my book," announced Albert once they'd finished.

"Make sure you put a jumper on or at least a scarf. It is December and I don't want you catching a cold," said his mother.

The little mouse ran upstairs and opened his clothes cupboard.

"Hmmm, now which one shall I wear," he said, looking at the various coloured jumpers that were neatly folded in the drawer. "The red one, I think, after all, it is nearly Christmas."

The little mouse pulled the jumper over his head and then went downstairs and into the garden. He sat down on the bench and continued reading his woodwork book.

"That's a very Christmassy jumper!" said a voice over the garden wall.

"Oh, hello, Mrs Saunders," said Albert. "Yes, I thought I'd better stay warm."

"Very wise, Albert. It is getting surprisingly colder around here. We may even get snow!" said Mrs Saunders. "Anyway, I see you're reading the book I loaned to you, are you enjoying it?"

"I am. I'd love to have a workshop but I don't think my mother will allow it. She says we don't have the room," sighed the little mouse.

"Oh dear, I sense a very sad mouse," said Mrs Saunders. "I'm afraid to say that your mother may be right, workshops can take up a lot of space. I mean, just look at Father Christmas."

"Father Christmas?" asked Albert.

"Yes, he has a huge workshop in Lapland where he makes all the Christmas toys for the children."

"Wow!" said Albert. "Really?"

"He certainly does."

Mrs Saunders then paused.

"Well, when I say he, what I mean is that his helpers make the toys. After all, he couldn't make all the toys for all the children in the entire world all by himself. That would be impossible," Mrs Saunders added.

"Is Lapland far?" asked Albert.

"I'll say. It's near the North Pole and very cold," she said. "Anyway, I'd better be getting back to the bookshop."

With that Mrs Saunders was gone, leaving Albert's mind full of thoughts.

Chapter 3

"Afternoon," said Big Tony as he swooped down into the garden and landed on the bench. "Nice jumper!"

"Thanks! Big Tony, did you know that Father Christmas has a workshop?"

"Yes, it's in Lapland near the North Pole and it's very cold," said Big Tony.

Albert looked curiously at his friend.

"You were listening, weren't you?"

The gull nodded his head and chuckled.

"But, jokes aside, I did know about his workshop," said Big Tony.

"Why didn't you tell me?" asked Albert.

"I thought you knew," said the gull.

Just then Mrs Mouse opened the front door.

"Would either of you boys like a mug of hot chocolate?" she asked.

"Yes, please!" said Albert.

"Not for me, thank you," said Big Tony. "I'm a bit full from lunch."

When Albert's mother had gone back inside the house the little mouse turned to his friend.

"So, this North Pole, where is it?" he asked.

"To be honest, I'm not really sure, but it's a long way, that I do know," he said.

"Hmm," thought Albert. "Would we need to fly there, or could we catch the train? No wait, we could go in the boat!"

"Now just slow down my little buddy," said the gull. "We don't even have an address for this place!"

7

"What place?' asked Mrs Mouse as she came out of the house with Albert's mug of hot chocolate.

Chapter 4

"Oops! Got to go," said Big Tony, and off he flew.

Mrs Mouse looked at her son.

"Albert Mouse, what place?" she demanded sternly.

"Erm, I was, well, when I say I, what I mean is Big Tony...," Albert stuttered.

"You are NOT having a workshop, so before you plan to visit any shops that sell tools, benches or wood, you can just forget it!" she said.

"It wasn't about buying workshop stuff, I promise," said Albert knowing he wasn't really telling a lie.

"So, why did Big Tony disappear so quickly then? He always does that when you two are up to something," said his mother.

"We were just discussing Christmas if you must know, and presents," said Albert again trying to be as honest as he could.

"I see, well, that's all it had better be, Albert Mouse," she said looking sternly at her son again. "Now, drink your hot chocolate before it gets cold."

Albert warmed his hands on the outside of the mug and smelt the chocolate steam before taking a sip.

"Mum, when I've finished this I'm going to take the woodwork book back to Mrs Saunders if that's ok?"

"Ok, but please don't be a nuisance," said his mother.

"I know," sighed Albert. "She has a shop to run."

When Albert had finished his hot

chocolate he picked up the book and headed off to see Mrs Saunders.

Chapter 5

The little mouse pushed open the door of the Dartmouth Community Bookshop.

"Hello, I've brought your book back! I was wondering if I can borrow one on Father Christmas and an atlas if you have one?" said Albert.

"Let me see. I have an atlas but I'm not sure if we have a book on Father Christmas," said Mrs Saunders, placing the woodwork book back on the shelf. "What is it you want to know about him?"

"I was talking to Big Tony and he

said Father Christmas lives in Lapland near the North Pole," said Albert.

"Big Tony is absolutely right, Father Christmas does live in Lapland," replied Mrs Saunders.

"Do you know if I can get the train there from Kingswear?" asked Albert.

Mrs Saunders laughed.

"Albert, Lapland is thousands of miles away in another country altogether. Much too far away for you to go to, I'm afraid to say."

"Oh," said Albert disappointedly.

"First, you need some very warm clothes," added Mrs Saunders, seeing how sad the little mouse looked.

"I have a jumper and a warm scarf," said Albert looking a bit happier.

"I think you'd need more than that. Even Father Christmas has to wear a big fur coat and boots. Anyway, you'd also need a passport," said Mrs Saunders.

"Passport?" asked Albert.

"It's a small book with your name and photograph in it that tells people who you are and where you're from."

"Couldn't I just tell them who I am? I'm sure they've probably heard of me," suggested Albert.

"I'm not sure that would be enough. Anyway, why do you want to go there?" she asked.

"I heard he has a huge workshop and I'd like to see it," said Albert.

"Yes, he does, and that's where all the toys are made for the children all over the world," said Mrs Saunders.

Just then, Albert heard his mother calling him.

"Oh, I'd better go. Thank you for the atlas, and all the information on Father Christmas," said Albert as he rushed out of the door and back to his house.

Chapter 6

Albert scrambled under the gate and hurried into the house.

"Yes, Mum?" he said as he went into the lounge.

"Albert, you mustn't disturb Mrs Saunders so much, she does have a shop to run," said Mrs Mouse. "What book have you borrowed now?"

"It's an atlas. I just need to see how far it is to Lapland where Father Christmas lives," said Albert laying down on the carpet and opening the large book.

"I can't believe that you still think

Father Christmas is real," giggled Dorothy.

"He IS real!" said Albert. "Mrs Saunders told me that he has a huge workshop where he makes toys for children all over the world at Christmas. I'm going there with Big Tony to help him make them."

"The only thing you have ever made is a nuisance of yourself," laughed Dorothy.

"That's quite enough Dorothy. I'm sure Albert would be very good at making toys and Father Christmas would be very grateful for the extra help. Now, if you want to make yourself useful you can go and make Albert and me a nice mug of hot chocolate!" said Mrs Mouse.

After Dorothy had gone into the kitchen the little mouse turned to his mother.

"Mum, do you think Yvonne at Hip Hip Hooray could make me a very warm jacket to keep me warm when I go to Lapland?" he asked.

"I'm sure she could, but let's find out how far Lapland is first shall we?" said Mrs Mouse. "Anyway, I really don't want you going on your own."

"It's okay, Big Tony is coming too," said Albert.

Chapter 7

As Albert sipped his hot chocolate, he turned page after page of the atlas looking for a place called Lapland.

"Look, Millie, Dartmouth's greatest explorer can't even find Lapland," laughed Dorothy as she watched her brother studying the atlas.

"Found it!" yelled Albert, excitedly pointing to a place with his finger.

"Really!?" asked Millie.

"Yes, it's here in a country called Finland. See, Dorothy, I am really a great explorer," he smiled.

"And where are we?" asked Millie looking at the atlas.

"Here!" said Albert, pointing to the southwest tip of the United Kingdom.

"Wow, it does look a long way," said his sister.

"It's quite far, but I'm sure it won't be a problem for me and Big Tony, after all, we do have a boat, and we can just sail around here," said Albert, moving his finger across the expanse of blue on the map.

Satisfied he had the route planned he sat up and took another sip of his hot chocolate.

"I think you should first write to Father Christmas and ask if he needs your help before you start planning a sea voyage," suggested Mrs Mouse.

"Good idea!" said Albert, closing the atlas and rushing off to his bedroom.

"Oh, bless him," giggled Dorothy. "He really thinks Father Christmas is real, doesn't he, Mum?"

"As I recall, you wrote to Father Christmas once and asked for a little brother," said Mrs Mouse.

"I never did!" replied Dorothy.

Mrs Mouse just smiled at her daughter.

Chapter 8

In his bedroom, Albert sat down at his desk, took a piece of paper from the drawer, and picked up his pen.

The little mouse then stared at the blank sheet of paper.

"Now, do I call him Father Christmas?" said Albert. "No, I need to be respectful."

Albert then wrote 'Dear Mr Christmas' at the top of the page.

He was staring out of the window, thinking of what to write next, when Big Tony suddenly appeared on the window ledge.

"Hey, Albert, what are you up to?' he asked.

"Hi, Big Tony. I'm just writing a letter to Father Christmas to ask if it will be okay for you and me to visit him in Lapland and see his workshop," said Albert. "But I'm struggling with how to start the letter."

"I'd start with 'Dear Mr Christmas' if it was me," said the gull trying to be helpful.

"That's what I thought," said the little mouse. "It's the next bit I'm having issues with."

The gull stepped onto the windowsill, jumped across, and landed on Albert's desk. He then settled himself down and scratched his beak.

"Ok, let me think," said the gull. "Got it! Write this down."

Albert steadied his pen in readiness.

"....Albert and I have been admirers of your work for many years," said Big

Tony. "No, wait, since you're writing the letter you'd better change that to Big Tony and I."

Albert scrunched up the paper and threw it in his waste paper basket. He then took a fresh sheet of paper and began scribbling.

"Now, where was I?" asked the gull. "Oh yes, the amazing, the incredible, and not to mention very smart Big Tony and I have been admirers of your work for many years. As you may be aware we are quite well known in Dartmouth for our good deeds. It was the two of us who single-handily captured Mickey Mustard. Anyway, the reason for this letter is to ask if it would be possible for me and Big Tony to come to Lapland and visit your workshop...."

Big Tony paused and looked at Albert.

"How long do you think we want to go for?" he asked.

Albert thought for a few moments before answering.

"A few days I should think, at least," he said.

"Good. So write that down," said the gull.

Chapter 9

The two friends spent the rest of the afternoon writing their letter to Father Christmas until eventually it was finished.

"Phew, I'm glad it's done, I've never written such a long letter," said Albert stretching his little fingers. "My hand is quite sore."

The little mouse signed the letter, folded it up and placed it in an envelope.

He then looked at his friend.

"What?" asked Big Tony.

"Do you know Father Christmas's address?" he asked.

"Well, there can't be many people in Lapland called Christmas so I'd just address it to Mr F. Christmas, The Workshop, Lapland," said Big Tony.

Albert quickly wrote the address down in big letters on the front of the envelope.

"There, now we need to post it," he said getting down from his chair.

"Right, I think I'll head off and get some food then. This letter writing is hungry work," said the gull, hopping onto the windowsill. With a flap of his wings, he was gone.

Albert put his hat and scarf on and went downstairs.

"Mum, I'm just posting my letter to Father Christmas. I'll be back in a moment," said the little mouse, as he put on his coat.

"Ok, but don't be long. It's getting cold out there," said his mother.

Chapter 10

Albert ran down the path, under the gate and out into the street.

There were a lot of people going about their Christmas shopping, carrying bags of presents.

"Sorry, excuse me. Coming through," said Albert squeezing past the shoppers as he headed in the direction of the Post Office.

"Gosh, the crowds out there are horrible," said the little mouse as he reached the counter and saw Mrs Tait.

"They get worse every year," she

said. "Anyway, it's really nice to see you, Albert. How can I help?"

"I'd just like to post this letter to Father Christmas," said the little mouse, pushing the envelope across the counter.

Mrs Tait looked at the address and picked up her pen.

"I'll just write Finland on this as well, just to make sure it gets there, ok?" she said.

"Oops, sorry! It's just Big Tony and I were in such a rush to get it in the post we forgot about that."

"It's fine. Is it your Christmas list to him?" she asked as she put a stamp on it.

"No, we are asking if we can go and visit him and see his workshop," said Albert.

"Wow, well, good luck! But you'll both need some very warm clothes," said Mrs Tait.

Albert nodded.

"That's what Mrs Saunders at the bookshop said. By the way, how's Bobby?"

"Oh, he's fine. He might be coming down to Dartmouth for Christmas which will be nice."

"Well if I'm not with Father Christmas you must bring him round to the house for a mince pie and hot chocolate," said Albert.

"That's very kind of you, Albert. Bobby would like that very much," said Mrs Tait with a smile.

"Right, well, I'd better go and brave the crowds again. Nice to see you, Mrs Tait."

"You too, Albert. Merry Christmas!"

"Merry Christmas," said the little mouse and he scurried out into the street.

Chapter 11

Albert managed to dodge all the shoppers on the way back home and squeeze back under the gate.

"Where do all these people come from," he asked himself as he walked back up the path to his front door.

"I'm home, Mum," he said as he hung his coat back up on the hook and took his hat and scarf off.

"Was the Post Office busy?" asked his mother.

"Not overly. Mrs Tait said her grandson might be coming to stay with her at Christmas so I've invited them for mince pies. That's if I'm still going to be here," said Albert as he warmed his hands next to the fire.

"Still going to be here?" asked his mother, looking surprised.

"If I've not gone to Lapland to see Father Christmas, Mum! Don't tell me you've forgotten about my trip?" said Albert.

"Yes, well, let's see what Father Christmas says first. He might not need your help," said Mrs Mouse.

"Oh no!" Albert said, slapping his forehead with his paw.

"What is it now?" asked his mother.

"I forgot to go and see Yvonne at Hip Hip Hooray to ask if she could make Big Tony and me some extra warm jackets for our trip."

"Oh, Albert, please wait to see if you get a reply from Father Christmas before you start bothering Yvonne for warm jackets. I'm sure she is very busy preparing for Christmas with her family and doesn't need you and Big Tony troubling her."

Albert didn't reply, but simply opened the atlas again and studied the best route to Lapland, while his mother went back to her knitting.

Chapter 12

Later that evening, the little mouse changed into his pyjamas and climbed into bed. After he had fluffed up his pillow, he pulled up his duvet and snuggled down to sleep.

His mother opened his bedroom door.

"Are you all ready?" she asked.

The little mouse nodded.

"Sleep well then. I'll see you in the morning," said his mother.

"Mum, I really hope Father Christmas replies to my letter soon," said Albert.

"I'm sure he will. Now you just sleep well and I'll see you in the morning," said his mother as she kissed him on the top of his head.

"Goodnight," said Albert closing his eyes.

The little mouse gradually drifted off to sleep and soon fell into a deep dream ....

Chapter 13

"Brrr! It's cold out there," said a strange voice.

Albert sat up in bed, rubbed his eyes and looked again.

"Is that.... really you!?" exclaimed Albert, looking at the strange figure who was dusting snow off his large red coat.

"Yes, it's me, Albert. I received your letter and thought I'd pop over to collect you. My sleigh will be far quicker than your boat."

The little mouse didn't know what to say so he just sat on his bed staring at

Father Christmas in equal shock and delight.

"Come on, come on, don't just sit there, put this on," said Father Christmas holding out a little red coat with white fur on the cuffs and hood. "It's freezing out there and I don't want your mother getting cross with me because you've caught a cold."

Albert jumped out of bed and quickly got dressed. He put the red coat on and buttoned it up.

"Ready?" asked Father Christmas.

"Yes," said Albert. "Oh, hang on, I'd better leave a note for my mother or she'll be worried."

"It's fine, I'll have you back in the morning before she wakes up," said Father Christmas.

"Wait!" said Albert. "We need to get Big Tony."

"All taken care of. He's already in the sleigh waiting for us."

Albert started walking toward his bedroom door.

"Albert, where are you going? It's this way," said Father Christmas, pointing to the fireplace in the corner of the bedroom.

"Of course! Right, I forgot," said the little mouse and followed Father Christmas up the chimney.

It was a bit of a scramble but soon Albert and Father Christmas emerged out of the chimney and onto the roof.

"Wow!" said Albert as he saw the big sleigh parked on his roof.

"This is Dasher, Dancer, Prancer, Vixen, Comet, Cupid, Dunder, Blixem and Rudolph," said Father Christmas as he introduced Albert to the nine reindeer. "And you know Big Tony!"

"Wow, can you believe this?!" Albert asked his friend as he climbed into the sleigh and sat down next to Big Tony.

"It is pretty exciting, I have to say!"

replied the gull, who was also wrapped up in a red jacket like Albert's.

"Ready?" asked Father Christmas, taking hold of the reins of the sleigh.

"Ready!" said the two friends excitedly, holding onto each other.

"Hold tight then, my friends!" said Father Christmas flicking the reins once.

The nine reindeer threw their heads back and took off into the night sky. Soon the town of Dartmouth was far below and disappearing into the distance.

Chapter 14

After a few minutes, Father Christmas turned to his two new friends.

"Are you enjoying this?" he asked, smiling from ear to ear.

"Definitely!" said Big Tony, excitedly.

"What about you, Albert? Is it better than your trip with those balloons"

"Absolutely! A million times more!" replied Albert. "But how do they manage to fly?" he said, pointing at the reindeer.

"It's really just a combination of antlaerodynamics, Elf Dust and my special blend of magical reindeer food," explained Father Christmas. "Now, who is ready for a nice cup of hot chocolate?"

"Oh, yes please!" grinned Big Tony. "I wouldn't mind a pasty too if you have one?"

"Good! Hold on to these, Albert," said Father Christmas, handing the reins to the little mouse.

He then reached under a blanket and brought out a large picnic basket.

"There you are, Big Tony, one extra large pasty."

Father Christmas took three mugs from the basket and a large flask.

"Hold them steady, Albert. I don't want to spill hot chocolate all over my nice coat otherwise Mrs Christmas will not be happy."

The little mouse did his best to keep the reindeer steady as the sleigh flew through the air.

"Nice work, Albert. Are you sure

you've not driven a sleigh before?" asked Father Christmas.

"No, it's my first time," replied the little mouse, feeling terribly pleased that Father Christmas thought he was doing such a good job.

Soon the three friends were drinking their hot chocolate as the sleigh made its way through the starry sky.

"How long will it take to get to Lapland?" asked Albert.

"Two seconds, I'll just find out," said Father Christmas, standing up and calling to the reindeer. "Rudolph, what's our ETA please?"

"What does ETA mean?" Albert whispered in Big Tony's ear.

"No idea!"

"It means estimated time of arrival," answered Father Christmas as he waited for the lead reindeer to make his calculations.

"Seven minutes!" shouted Rudolph.

"Right, well, we had better finish our drinks, pack the basket away and prepare for our landing," said Father Christmas.

He then took a mobile phone out of his coat pocket.

"Hello, this is Father Christmas. ETA seven minutes. Albert Mouse and Big Tony are on board. Please switch on the runway lights. Over and out."

Albert looked into the darkness but couldn't see anything and wondered if there was a problem.

Chapter 15

Even Big Tony was getting slightly worried as he peered into the darkness.

Then, all of a sudden, two rows of white lights appeared dimly in the distance. And then, as if by magic, lights of every possible colour began to swirl all around them like fireflies.

"Is that....?"

"Yes, Albert, welcome to Lapland," beamed Father Christmas.

"Wow! I've never seen so many lights in my whole life," whispered Albert in complete awe.

Just then a red light began to flash on the dashboard of the sleigh.

"What does that mean?" asked Big Tony pointing to the warning light and looking worried.

"Don't worry! It's just my safety system telling us to put our seat belts on and prepare for landing," chuckled Father Christmas.

Albert and Big Tony quickly fastened their seat belts.

Gradually the sleigh reduced its speed. The runway lights got closer and closer, until, eventually, the sleigh gently touched down on the snow.

"Well done everyone!" clapped Father Christmas, thanking the reindeer as the sleigh came to a stop.

"Can you believe it, Big Tony!? We are actually here in Lapland," said Albert, hardly able to contain his excitement.

"I can't believe I've just been given a

pasty by Father Christmas!" exclaimed the gull.

Father Christmas took the harnesses of the reindeer, then went to the back of the sleigh and came back with a large sack.

"Are those presents for the children?" asked Albert.

Father Christmas laughed.

"No, Albert, they're carrots for the reindeer. You can help me if you'd like."

Albert and Big Tony happily fed the carrots to the reindeer and thanked them heartily for their efforts. Soon the sack was empty.

"Right, let's introduce you to everyone," said Father Christmas. "Follow me!"

Chapter 16

Albert and Big Tony followed Father Christmas across the snow to a large house made of wooden logs.

"I'm home, dear," called Father Christmas as he opened the door.

Father Christmas turned to Albert and Big Tony.

"Here, let me take your coats. Now, go and warm yourself next to the fire," he said.

As the two friends took their coats off a very friendly-looking older lady appeared.

"You were quick, dear," she said, as

she kissed her husband on the cheek and then looked at the two visitors.

"And you two must be Big Tony and Albert. We've heard so much about you," she smiled. "Let me introduce myself. I'm Mrs Christmas."

"I'm very pleased to meet you," said Albert smiling widely.

"You have a lovely home, Mrs Christmas," said Big Tony, his eyes wide open as he took in the wonderful sight that had greeted them both.

"Thank you. It does us comfortably. Now, can I get you anything to eat? I've got some lovely pasties that have just come out of the oven."

"Ooh, yes please!" said the two friends in tandem.

Mrs Christmas went into the kitchen and was soon back carrying three plates.

"Here we go," she said.

Albert, Big Tony and Father Christmas sat and ate their pasties.

"So, Albert, how is your mother?" asked Mrs Christmas.

"She's very well, thank you," said Albert, trying not to talk with his mouth full.

"And your Grandma Bramble?"

"She's fine too. We saw her last Christmas," said Albert.

"And what about you, Big Tony? I heard you learnt to swim?" asked Mrs Christmas.

Big Tony almost choked on his pasty.

"I did, but how did you know about that!?" he exclaimed.

Father Christmas chuckled loudly.

"I'm Father Christmas, Big Tony, we see everything that goes on in every home. We see who has been good and who hasn't. And let me tell you, we've been very impressed by you two, haven't we, dear?"

Mrs Christmas smiled and nodded.

"We know you've both made a few mistakes, like not telling your mother about the boat, but that is fine. After all, we all make mistakes, but it's what we do to say sorry or make amends that's important."

Albert and Big Tony both looked at each other and nodded.

"Anyway, do you two boys want to get some sleep? I've made up two beds in the spare room. You've got a busy day tomorrow," said Mrs Christmas.

"Yes please, I am a bit tired," said Albert yawning.

"Me too," yawned Big Tony.

Mrs Christmas showed the two friends to the spare bedroom.

Chapter 17

"Here you are," announced Mrs Christmas as she opened the bedroom door. "I hope you both like it?"

Albert and Big Tony stood and looked in amazement. They had never seen such a wonderful room in their entire lives. There were two single beds, and on each one was a pillow. One had a large 'AM' embroidered on it and on the other the letters 'BT'. Neatly folded on each bed was a set of tartan pyjamas and on the floor matching pairs of slippers.

"Wow, it looks like a Christmas card. It's so beautiful," said Albert as he looked around the room.

"You have your own bathroom and if you need anything you just let me know. Sleep well and we will see you in the morning."

Mrs Christmas quietly closed the door behind her.

The two friends looked at each other.

"Can you believe this place, Albert?" said Big Tony. "Look, even the dressing gown has my initials on it!"

The little mouse opened the bathroom door and looked inside.

"Big Tony, the towels have our names on them too!"

"I LOVE this place," replied the gull, as he changed into his pyjamas and slid his feet into his slippers.

Soon the two friends were in their beds having cleaned their teeth.

"Isn't this the most amazing adventure ever?" said Albert, and he put his hands behind his head and looked around the room.

"It sure is, Albert."

The two friends fell asleep.

Chapter 18

The smell of cooked breakfast slowly crept under the bedroom door and reached the bed where Big Tony was still sleeping.

Suddenly the gull sat bolt upright, opened one eye and looked around. He then opened the other eye.

"Food!" he exclaimed and looked across at Albert.

The little mouse turned over and his nose began to twitch as he smelt the eggs, toast and sausages. He then opened one eye and looked at Big Tony who was already out of bed and putting his dressing gown on as he walked to the bathroom.

Albert slowly sat up, yawned and stretched his little arms.

"How did you sleep, Big Tony?" he asked.

"Like a log," mumbled Big Tony, who was obviously cleaning his teeth.

"Me too. I think it was the excitement of the sleigh ride," said Albert, as he put his dressing gown on and joined his friend in the bathroom.

"Look, even the soap has our names on it," said the gull pointing to the small dish that had a purple bar of lavender soap on it.

"My Mum would love this place, lavender is her favourite....."

The little mouse stopped mid-sentence.

"Mum!" he shouted and ran out of the bathroom.

The gull quickly rinsed the toothpaste from his mouth.

"What is it, Albert? What's wrong?" asked Big Tony.

"Oh no, this is terrible! We are in so much trouble," said Albert as he flung the bedroom door open.

"Father Christmas! Father Christmas!" he called.

Chapter 19

Father Christmas, who was sitting in a large armchair reading the newspaper looked up.

"Albert, what's wrong?" he asked.

"You need to take us home straight away! Oh, I'm going to be in so much trouble," cried the little mouse.

"What, now?" asked Father Christmas, looking surprised.

"Yes, this instant! Before my mother wakes up!" said Albert panicking.

"Ahh, I see. I should have explained something to you last night before you went to bed."

"Explained what?" asked the little mouse, looking even more worried.

"What's happened?" asked Mrs Christmas as she came out of the kitchen with two plates of breakfast.

"I need to go home right away," said Albert "Before my mother sees I'm gone. Oh no, she will be so worried."

Mrs Christmas looked at her husband.

"You forgot to tell him, didn't you?" she said.

Father Christmas nodded his head slowly.

"Tell me what?" asked Albert beginning to cry.

"Albert, time here passes very differently than where you live. Hours in the real world are sometimes days in this magical place," said Mrs Christmas, soothing Albert.

The little mouse looked confused.

"That's how we get so many toys made in time for Christmas," said

Father Christmas. "One hour in your world can be a whole day in mine! If we leave tonight after supper, we can get you home long before your mother wakes up."

Albert stopped crying.

"Really? So, I'm not in trouble?" asked Albert, drying his tears on the sleeve of his dressing gown.

"And that means we don't have to leave now and miss breakfast?" asked Big Tony, looking relieved. "Phew."

Father Christmas got out of his chair, walked over to the dresser and picked up a snow globe and shook it.

"Albert, come here and look," he said. "When the snow settles look into the globe and tell me what you see."

The little mouse peered into the glass ball.

"Is that my Mum?" asked Albert, hardly able to believe his eyes.

Father Christmas nodded and smiled.

"She's fast asleep and do you see the clock on her bedside table?"

Albert moved his head closer to the glass ball.

"It says seven minutes past eleven," said the mouse.

"See, nothing to worry about," chuckled Father Christmas. "Now let's have breakfast before it goes cold. We have lots to do today."

"I'm starving!" said Big Tony pulling out a chair at the table and sitting down.

Albert hurried back into the bedroom and changed out of his pyjamas into his trousers and shirt, then hurried back to the table feeling much happier.

Chapter 20

Albert hadn't realised how hungry he was and soon his plate was empty.

"That was delicious, thank you very much," said the little mouse wiping his mouth with a napkin.

"You are very welcome," smiled Mrs Christmas.

"Yes, that's really filled me up, well, for a few hours anyway," said Big Tony.

"Right, are you both ready to see the workshop?" asked Father Christmas getting up from the table.

"Definitely!" said Albert with a big smile.

After they had all put on their warm coats, the two friends followed Father Christmas outside.

"Crikey, there's so much snow," said Albert, almost disappearing with his first step.

"I think I'd better help you," said Father Christmas and with that, he picked the little mouse up and placed him in the pocket of his red coat.

Father Christmas walked over to a large wooden building and pushed the door open.

"Wow!" said Albert as he looked about.

There were benches everywhere and at each bench was an elf, either sawing, painting, drilling or hammering. Other elves were running about, so fast that they were almost a blur. And there were toys everywhere!

"Good morning everyone! Stop what you're doing, please. I'd like you all to meet Albert and Big Tony," said Father

Christmas taking Albert out of his pocket and placing him down on a bench.

"Hello everyone!" said Albert waving.

Immediately the elves all gathered around the bench to look at Albert and Big Tony.

"Let me introduce you to the main Elf Team. This is Alabaster Snowball, he has two degrees from Cambridge. He is the Administrator of the "Naughty or Nice List", so you definitely want to be on his side. Then this is Bushy Evergreen, my engineer and inventor of my magic toy-making machine. Here is Pepper Minstix who is the protector of my magic world, and Head of Elf Security."

"Pleased to meet you," said Albert, shaking their hands.

"Next we have Shinny Upatree. He is my oldest elf, even older than me. Shinny is the leader of all the Elves.

Then this is Sugarplum Mary. Mary is in charge of sweets and chocolates."

"I'll need to talk to you later," said Big Tony, smiling and shaking her hand.

"Lastly we have Wunorse Openslae. Wunorse is about six hundred years old. Because of his Viking ancestors, he is in charge of the reindeer, but he is also one of my best inventors and dreams up lots of new toys. He invented and built my sleigh."

Father Christmas looked around at the hundreds of other faces in the room.

"The rest of the elves you'll get to know throughout the day."

"Albert and I are very pleased to meet you all," said Big Tony.

"Father Christmas, what would you like me and Big Tony to do?" asked Albert, eager to help the elves.

Father Christmas took two sheets of paper out of his coat and handed one to Albert and the other to Big Tony.

"Oh excellent, a wooden train!" said Albert excitedly.

Big Tony looked at his drawing.

"Brilliant, a plane!" he said, looking happy.

"Find yourself a bench each. You'll find all the wood you need over there and paint is in the finishing room," said Father Christmas.

The two friends quickly found a bench and got to work.

Chapter 21

Albert was pleased he had been given a train to make and once he had studied the plans he chose the wood he needed.

"How are getting on?" asked Wunorse Openslae.

"I'm good, thank you," said Albert as he started cutting the shapes out of wood.

"Your cutting is very good, do you have a workshop where you live?" asked Wunorse.

"No, but I'm hoping to get one soon if my Mum lets me," said Albert.

"Well, you're doing really well. If you need any help just call me."

Over at the other bench, Big Tony was also cutting the various parts of his plane when Sugarplum Mary appeared.

"Would you like some chocolate sweets, Big Tony? It's my new recipe," she said.

Big Tony took a chocolate sweet and popped it into his mouth.

"Oh my, that is delicious," said the gull. "May I please have another one, Sugarplum?"

Sugarplum Mary smiled, nodded and left the bowl on Big Tony's bench before returning to the kitchen.

"Albert, how are you getting on?" shouted Big Tony taking another piece of chocolate from the bowl and putting it in his mouth.

"Good," replied the little mouse. "I've cut all the pieces out, now I just need to glue them together and then make the wheels. You?"

"Same. I'm just about to use the glue," said Big Tony.

All around the workshop the elves were hard at work making all sorts of toys of every description.

Suddenly a bell started to ring.

"What's that?" asked Albert looking around.

"I hope it's not the fire alarm," said Big Tony, grabbing the rest of the chocolates.

"Lunchtime!" shouted Pepper Minstix.

"What, already?" asked Albert.

"Excellent!" said Big Tony.

The gull and the little mouse followed the rest of the elves into the dining room and sat down at the long table. At one end sat Mrs Christmas and at the other end sat Father Christmas. The table was covered with more food than either Big Tony or Albert had seen.

"Albert, how are you getting on with that train?' asked Mrs Christmas as she poured some gravy onto her roast potatoes.

"Very well, thank you!" said Albert. "I should be able to start painting it after lunch."

"Wonderful!" smiled Mrs Christmas.

Chapter 22

A short time later Albert and Big Tony were full of the most wonderful food ever. They couldn't eat one more Brussels sprout, any more spoons of Cauliflower Cheese or bowls of Christmas Pudding. Even Big Tony had to admit that he was full which was a surprise to everyone.

After helping Mrs Christmas clear the table everyone went back to work.

Albert stood by his bench, looked at the plans and scratched his head.

"Is everything ok, Albert? You look confused?" asked Wunorse Openslae.

"I am a bit," replied the little mouse. "I'm just about to start painting and I can't see any paint colour instructions."

The elf chuckled.

"You won't. We just paint the toys any colour we want," said Wunorse. "Just choose your favourite colours."

"Oh, amazing! That's such fun" said Albert looking relieved.

"Oh, one other thing," said Wunorse. "Remember to paint your name underneath the train to say you made it. I've told Big Tony to do the same."

"Got it!' said Albert, picking up his train and hurrying off to the paint shop.

When Albert had finished painting his train red, green and black he carefully wrote 'Made by Albert Mouse' on the train.

"Something is missing," mused the little mouse as he looked at his finished train.

After a few moments, he realised what it was.

"Of course! The train needs a name," he said, painting a name on both sides of the toy.

"How are you getting on, Albert?" asked Father Christmas as he came into the paint shop.

"I've finished!" said the little mouse, feeling very pleased with himself.

Father Christmas bent down and closely inspected the train.

"Well, I have to say, Albert, I'm very impressed with your craftsmanship," he said eventually. "Giving the train a name is also a very nice touch. I like it a lot."

"Thank you. I've named it Goliath, the same as the train back in Kingswear," said Albert. "And I've written my name underneath as Wunorse told me to."

"Perfect!" said Father Christmas.

Just then Big Tony brought his plane into the paint shop.

"Wow! Your plane looks excellent," said Albert.

"Thanks," said Big Tony, feeling proud. "Your train looks amazing too. This has been such good fun."

Albert smiled in agreement.

"I'd better go and tidy my bench up," said the little mouse as he skipped happily back to the main workshop.

Chapter 23

Big Tony had soon finished painting his wooden plane and stood back nervously as Father Christmas inspected the workmanship.

"Another good job!" he exclaimed, patting the gull on the back.

"Thanks!" said Big Tony looking very pleased with himself.

"And did you remember to write your name underneath?" asked Father Christmas.

Big Tony nodded.

"Excellent!" said Father Christmas looking at his watch. "Well, you've both finished making your toys so quickly that I might as well make plans to get you both home now."

"I have to clean my bench first but I shouldn't be too long," said the gull and hurried back to the workshop.

"Albert, Father Christmas says he'll take us home since we've both finished making our toys," said Big Tony.

Once their benches were clean the two friends said thank you and goodbye to all their new elf friends.

"We must also go and say goodbye to Mrs Christmas," said Albert.

"Yes, you must. I'll get the reindeer and the sleigh ready. I'll see you in about five minutes," said Father Christmas.

At the house, Mrs Christmas was very sad to say goodbye.

"Here, I've made you each a pasty for the journey," she said handing Albert a carrier bag. "There are only two because my husband will have his supper when he gets back home."

Mrs Christmas hugged the two boys and kissed them both on their heads.

"Thank you for everything, Mrs Christmas,' said Big Tony.

"You are both very welcome," said Mrs Christmas with a tear in her eye.

"We'd better go now, Father Christmas is waiting," said Albert, and the two friends went out across the snow to where the sleigh was waiting.

Albert took a few carrots out of the sack at the back of the sleigh and gave them to the reindeer.

"All ready?" asked Father Christmas, climbing aboard.

"Ready!" said Albert and Big Tony, sitting down on the seat and fastening their seatbelts.

"Let's go!" said Father Christmas and gently the reindeer pulled the sleigh into the air.

Albert and Big Tony waved to Mrs

Christmas and all the elves who had come outside to see them off.

Soon the lights of Father Christmas's home were far below them. Albert and Big Tony started to feel sad that their adventure to Lapland was over and that their new friends would be so far away. They looked at each other and smiled as they snuggled down in the back of the sleigh.

Chapter 24

As the sleigh raced through the sky, Albert suddenly remember the pasties Mrs Christmas had given him. He took one out and gave it to Big Tony.

"Father Christmas, would you like half of mine? I'm still a bit full from lunch, and I don't think I can eat a whole one," asked Albert.

"Oh, yes please, but don't tell Mrs Christmas or I'll be in trouble," chuckled Father Christmas.

Soon the lights of Dartmouth came into view and the reindeer began to slow down.

"Here we are," said Father Christmas. "It didn't take long did it?"

"Are you sure my Mum will still be asleep?" asked the little mouse suddenly worrying he would be in trouble.

"You have absolutely nothing to worry about," replied Father Christmas as the reindeer gently landed on the roof of No.10 Higher Street.

"Thank you so much, Father Christmas, this has been the most amazing adventure ever," said Albert, throwing his arms around the big red coat and hugging tightly.

"You are both most welcome," he replied, patting Albert on the head. "Do you want me to help you down the chimney or will you be alright?"

"I think I'll be fine," said the little mouse, as he and Big Tony climbed down from the sleigh.

Albert and Big Tony said goodbye to

the reindeer and then stood well back as Father Christmas waved goodbye.

The two friends watched and waved as the sleigh rose into the air and flew off back to Lapland.

"Wow, Albert, that was an amazing trip wasn't it?" said Big Tony. "I'm so glad we wrote that letter."

"Me too," yawned the little mouse. "Well, I suppose we'd better get to bed. Goodnight, Big Tony."

"Goodnight, Albert," said the gull.

The little mouse carefully climbed down the chimney into his bedroom. He stood quietly at his bedroom door and listened. When he was sure everyone was still asleep, Albert began to get changed out of his clothes and into his pyjamas.

He then looked at the alarm clock that was sitting on the table beside his bed.

"Four o'clock," said the little mouse.

"Just enough time to get some sleep."
And with that, he climbed into bed and
closed his eyes.....

Chapter 25

Albert was still asleep when a knock at his bedroom door woke him. The little mouse stretched his arms and legs, yawned and opened his eyes as his mother opened the door.

"I just need to collect your clothes for washing," said his mother as she picked up his pile of clothes that lay in a heap on the floor.

Albert stretched and yawned again.

"Someone's a sleepy head this morning," said his mother. "Did you have a good night's sleep?"

"I did. I dreamt I visited Father

Christmas with Big Tony. We were helping the elves make wooden toys for all the children around the world. It was very tiring," said the little mouse.

"I bet it was. Well, it's almost nine o'clock so you'd better get yourself out of bed. I don't want you wasting the whole day," said his mother as she left the room.

Albert pulled back the duvet and swung his legs over the edge of the bed. As he did, some sawdust fell onto the floor.

"I wonder where that came from? Oh well," said the little mouse scratching his head and putting his dressing gown on before going to the bathroom to clean his teeth and wash his face.

Chapter 26

Downstairs Mrs Mouse began sorting out Albert's clothes for the washing machine. As usual, she checked all the pockets to make sure her son hadn't left anything in them.

"That's a bit odd," said Mrs Mouse, as she turned out the pockets of Albert's trousers and some sawdust fell onto the floor.

Mrs Mouse picked up some of the wood dust in her hand, held it to her nose and sniffed.

"It smells like pine wood," she said, shaking her head with curiosity.

She picked up his jacket and two half-eaten carrots fell onto the floor.

Mrs Mouse shook her head again as she placed the carrots on the kitchen table.

"Sometimes I really wonder what that boy gets up to. Half the time I blame Big Tony, but carrots, I give up with the pair of them," said Mrs Mouse placing Albert's clothes in the washing machine and closing the door.

Albert came downstairs and sat down at the table, still yawning.

"What's with the carrots, Mum?" he asked, picking up one of the half-eaten carrots.

"I thought you would tell me," said his mother.

"Me? They're not mine," said Albert, looking at the large teeth marks that were clearly visible on one of the carrots.

"Well, they were in your jacket pocket."

"Mine? Really?" replied the mouse looking surprised.

"Yes. Along with this sawdust that's all over the floor," said his mother.

"That's strange because there is sawdust on my bedroom floor also. Maybe we have woodworm?" suggested Albert.

"Nice try young man," said his mother. "I hope you haven't been secretly doing woodwork upstairs, because if you have I won't be happy."

"Definitely nothing to do with me," said the little mouse. "You can even ask Big Tony if you like."

"Oh, like he's Mr Honesty!"

"Big Tony is honest, Mum! You just don't know him as well as I do," said Albert as he poured himself a glass of milk.

"Well, after you've had your breakfast you can get a dustpan and brush, sweep up this sawdust and then go to your room and sweep up there," said his mother as she prepared a bowl of cereal for Albert's breakfast.

As Albert sat back down at the table his mother looked at him.

"What is it?" asked the little mouse, as he sipped his milk.

"You have red paint on your fur," said his mother, then she paused. "And green. And black. What have you been doing?" she demanded.

Albert looked at the paint.

"I'm not sure," he said looking confused.

"After you've eaten your breakfast and cleaned up this sawdust you're going straight in the bath young man," said his mother.

While the little mouse ate his cereal he tried to think how he had managed to get paint on himself.

It was all very odd.

Chapter 27

The days passed and soon Christmas arrived in Dartmouth. The streets were full of lights and decorations and shoppers were busy rushing about for last-minute gifts.

At No. 10 Higher Street, the Mouse family prepared their tree and put up the decorations and lights.

Albert had written and delivered all his Christmas cards. There was one for Mrs Saunders thanking her for letting him borrow her books. He wrote one for Theresa at the Dartmouth Visitor Centre and one for Yvonne at Hip Hip

Hooray who had made him his lovely Regatta jacket and swimming costume. There was one to Mr Britton, Dartmouth's Harbour Master and one to Daisy who had taught Albert to swim.

Albert felt sure he had remembered everyone and checked his Christmas card list more than once, just to make sure.

On Christmas Eve, before Albert went up to bed, the little mouse left a glass of milk and a mince pie out for Father Christmas. He then said goodnight to his mother and went upstairs.

The next morning Albert leapt out of bed and rushed downstairs into the lounge.

"Father Christmas has been!" he shouted, looking at the pile of presents that were laying in front of the fireplace.

He then looked at the empty glass

and the crumbs from the eaten mice pie.

"Yes, he's definitely been," said Albert with a smile.

"Father Christmas isn't real you know?" said Dorothy as she came into the lounge followed by Millie.

"He is so!" shouted Albert. "Look, he's eaten the mince pie I left for him and the glass is empty."

Dorothy shook her head and smiled at her sister.

"Isn't he sweet? He still believes in Father Christmas," she said.

Just then there was a knock at the door.

"Hey Albert, maybe that's Father Christmas to see you," laughed Dorothy.

Albert got up and went to the door.

Chapter 28

Albert opened the front door.

"No, it's ok," he shouted. "It's Big Tony."

"Merry Christmas!" said the gull, hugging his friend.

"Merry Christmas, Big Tony," said Albert. "Come on in, we're just about to open our presents.

Albert and Big Tony joined Dorothy and Millie in a circle on the carpet, while Mrs Mouse picked up each present and read out the name that had been written on the label.

"Now these are from me," said Mrs

Mouse passing the children a little parcel each.

Eagerly the children tore open their presents.

"What's this?" asked Dorothy, holding up a long knitted tube.

"It's a tail sock!" shouted Albert excitedly.

"Excellent!" screamed Millie.

"So that's what you've been knitting all this time," said Albert, smiling at his mother.

"Well I thought you needed something to keep your little tails warm in winter," said Mrs Mouse.

Soon all the presents had been opened. There were dolls and clothes for Dorothy and Millie. Mrs Mouse had received a new hat and a cookery book she had been looking at in Mrs Saunder's bookshop.

Big Tony received some vouchers for free meals at the Wheelhouse from Albert which he was very happy about.

Albert was extremely pleased with his presents, especially the new tweed cap from Big Tony.

When all the presents had been opened, Mrs Mouse gathered up all the torn wrapping paper and noticed two white envelopes and two unopened presents laying next to the fireplace.

"It seems there are two more here," she said and looked at the writing. "One is for Albert and one is for Big Tony but I don't recognise the writing."

Chapter 29

The little mouse took the present from his mother and looked at the label.

"I wonder who these are from?" Albert asked, quickly opening the present.

"It's a compass!" exclaimed Albert with great excitement.

"Who is it from?" asked Millie.

"I don't know," said Albert opening the envelope.

"Well?" asked Mrs Mouse.

"It's from Father Christmas!" beamed Albert.

"Yeah, right!" laughed Dorothy.

"Albert, read it," urged Millie, getting very excited.

Albert cleared his throat and began to read the card.

"I just wanted to say thank you for your long letter. It was so good of you to come to Lapland and help in my workshop. You did a wonderful job making the wooden train. I especially liked the colours you chose to paint it. Red, green and black are my favourite colours too. Your woodworking skills are outstanding and I hope you will both come and help us all again next Christmas. I hope you like the compass and may it guide you on your adventures. Merry Christmas to you and your family. PS. Dasher, Dancer, Prancer, Vixen, Comet, Cupid, Dunder, Blixem and Rudolph all send their love and thank you for the carrots."

"What, Rudolph the Red-Nosed Reindeer? " asked Millie.

"I guess," said Albert looking very confused.

He then turned and looked at Big Tony.

"What have you got?" he asked his friend.

Big Tony tore open his present.

"It's a telescope!" he said excitedly.

"Cool!" said Albert.

"Who's it from?" asked Millie.

Big Tony opened his card and read it out loud.

"Merry Christmas, Big Tony. I just wanted to say thank you for coming to Lapland with Albert. You certainly made a fantastic wooden plane and I'm sure the lucky child who receives it will be very happy. Please come and help us all again next Christmas. I hope you like the telescope which I know you will put to good use looking for unattended pasties and bags of chips. Merry Christmas to you!"

The gull looked at Albert.

"What's going on?' he asked.

"I'm not sure," said Albert, shrugging his shoulders.

"Let me read the card," said Dorothy, snatching the card from Big Tony and reading it.

"Well, it's obviously some kind of joke. Did you write this, Mum?" she asked.

"I certainly didn't, but I think we could all do with a hot chocolate and a mince pie," said Mrs Mouse getting up and going into the kitchen.

Chapter 30

Albert left his sisters to listen to Big Tony talk about the reindeer and went into the kitchen to talk to his mother.

"Mum, what is going on?" asked the little mouse.

"I don't know. It's all very strange, but it would account for all the sawdust, the half-eaten carrots and the paint," replied his mother as she put a pan of milk on the stove to warm up.

"But I thought I was just dreaming," said Albert.

"Some people say that when we sleep we really do go to those places in our dreams. Maybe that's what happened. To be honest, nothing surprises me anymore," said his mother as she put a spoonful of chocolate powder into each of the five mugs.

"Did I really go to Lapland?" asked the little mouse scratching his head.

"My mother always used to say to me that there is more in this world than we will ever understand. Maybe what happened in your dream is one of those things," said Albert's mother as she placed the mugs on a tray together with a box of mince pies.

Albert followed his mother back into the lounge.

———

In a home far away a little boy sat on the carpet with his family and unwrapped one of his Christmas presents.

"It's a wooden train!" said the little

boy excitedly. "It's just what I asked Father Christmas for."

The little boy turned the red, green and black train over and some writing caught his eye.

"What is it?" asked his mother.

"It says 'Made by Albert Mouse'," replied the little boy looking at his mother. "Do you think that's the real Albert Mouse? The one who lives in Dartmouth?"

"It might be," said his mother. "I shouldn't think there are too many people called Albert Mouse."

"Wow!" said the little boy, beaming from ear to ear.

Chapter 31

That night, as Albert lay in bed, he hoped he would dream of visiting Father Christmas again, but he didn't.

Instead, he dreamt that he and Big Tony sailed out of Dartmouth harbour and explored the world guided by the compass Father Christmas had given him.

For Albert that was just as good a dream as visiting Lapland.

I hope you have enjoyed reading about
my adventures with
Big Tony.
If you come to Dartmouth, please come
and visit my house.
You will probably see me in my
bedroom window.
You can also join The Albert Mouse
Society

Albert

Did you enjoy this book?

If you have enjoyed this book, then
please take a minute to leave a review.
You can also sign up to our blog to
receive updates on new books from
James Hywel.
https://jameshywel.com/blog

Thank you, Albert and I appreciate your
support!

Acknowledgments

I'm grateful to Brian and Pam, the human owners of Cherub Cottage, for sharing their house with Albert and his family.

Thank you to the people of Dartmouth for welcoming me into their vibrant town which holds an abundance of charm and seafaring history.

As always I am grateful to "Walter" for sending me the breeze that moves the willows.

About the Author

James Hywel is a children's author and creator of both Mr Milliner and Albert Mouse.

He is a member of The Royal Society of Literature, The Society of Authors and The Dartmouth and Kingswear Society.

For more books and updates visit our website:

www.jameshywel.com

Remember to sign up to our blog

https://jameshywel.com/blog

for news, new releases and giveaways.

Albert Mouse Esquire

Albert met with Sarah from Break the Cycle and decided he needed his own company name. He remembered receiving a letter that said *To Albert Mouse Esq.*

"Yes," he thought. "That's me!"

Albert Mouse Esq. helps children and young people benefit from bespoke educational programmes that support their development, helping them to navigate their thoughts and feelings, and appreciate their time in and out of school. Thus, supporting positive relationships and challenging negative behaviour.

Albert is excited to be visiting schools with his friend Sarah to talk to children who are feeling anxious, nervous, upset, worried or confused. Albert feels many of the same feelings as other children his age do.

www.albertmouseesquire.com

Part of Break The Cycle C.I.C.

Company Number 14265959

By Appointment to
children's imagination

www.jameshywel.com

Printed in Great Britain
by Amazon